The Little B[ook of] GIVING

HOLIDAY EDITION

By Zack Bush and Laurie Friedman
Illustrated by Sarah Van Evera

DEDICATED TO YOU —
OUR WONDERFUL, GIVING READER.
HAPPY HOLIDAYS!

THIS BOOK BELONGS TO:

_____

Holiday time is a special time! It means food, fun, family . . .

And **gifts**.

Sometimes when people think of a **gift** for the **holidays,** they only think of a present that comes wrapped up in a box with a bow.

But did you know there are many other kinds of **gifts** you can **give** to make the **holidays** extra special?

Gifts that don't cost money,
but that come straight from your heart.

Want to learn more?
Just turn the page!

You can draw a picture . . .

make a card . . .

or pick some beautiful flowers.

You can even surprise your
parents with a special meal.

These are just a few
things that you can **give**.
But there are so many more!

You can **give** the **gift** of friendship . . .

by including others who don't have anyone to play with.

You can **give** the **gift** of helping . . .

By pitching
in when someone
needs a hand.

You can **give** the **gift** of sharing . . .

By offering to **give** another person some of what you have.

You can **give** the **gift** of caring . . .

By visiting
someone who
is sick or hurt.

Any of these **gifts** will help make someone else's **holidays** a whole lot brighter!

You can also **give** the **gift** of listening.

One great way to do that is by paying attention while another person is talking.

You can **give** the **gift** of love.

When you **give** someone a special hug,
it shows them how much you care.

And you can **give** the **gift** of time to someone you love, just by being with them.

And if your someone is an animal, that counts too!

One of the most appreciated **gifts** you can **give** is your gratitude.

It is as simple as saying "thank you" or writing a note when someone does something nice for you.

Still not sure what you want
to **give** this **holiday** season?

How about
a song?

A story?

A special show?

Or a memory?

You can **give** the
gift of humor.

Making someone laugh by being silly
is always a good way to cheer a person up.

You can **give** the **gift** of community.

When you work with others,
it is easier to get things done.
Not only will it improve the world
around you, but it is also more
fun to work together than alone!

And you can **give** the **gift**
of volunteering.

Helping others in need is a truly wonderful
gift to **give**. Especially during the **holidays**!

Why is **giving** so important?

Because when you **give**, it shows other people that you care.

When is it a good
time to **give**?

It is always a good time
to **give** of yourself . . .
no matter which **holidays**
you celebrate.

Which **gifts** do you want
to give this **holiday** season?

KINDNESS

UNDERSTANDING

FRIENDSHIP

LOVE

JOY

Happiness

CARING

GENEROSITY

ENCOURAGEMENT

No matter what you choose,
when you **give**,
you will feel really good inside.

And so will everyone around you.

CONGRATULATIONS!

You've earned your GIVING BADGE.
Now you know so many great ways to make the
holidays extra special.

Go to the website
www.BooksByZackAndLaurie.com
to print out your giving badge.
And if you like this book,
please go to Amazon and
leave a kind review.

Keep reading all of the books in
#thelittlebookof
series to learn new things
and earn more badges.

Other books in the series:

The Little Book of Camping
The Little Book of Friendship
The Little Book of Kindness
The Little Book of Presidential Elections
The Little Book of Patience

Made in the USA
Coppell, TX
16 November 2020

41417560R00026